ISBN 1 85854 190 5
© Brimax Books Ltd 1996. All rights reserved.
Published by Brimax Books Ltd, Newmarket, England CB8 7AU, 1996.
Printed in France - n°70013.

The Artist wishes to thank the Kneehigh Theatre, Driftwood Spars, and
the St. Agnes Pirates.

TREASURE ISLAND

ROBERT LOUIS STEVENSON

Adapted by John Escott

ILLUSTRATED BY NEIL REED

BRIMAX • NEWMARKET • ENGLAND

Treasure Island

Treasure Island was first published in 1883. It is a tale of high adventure that has thrilled and captured the imagination of generations of children and adults. Although Robert Louis Stevenson wrote several very popular novels, *Treasure Island* was by far his most successful.

Treasure Island tells the story of young Jim Hawkins. He leaves England with his friends, Squire Trelawney and Doctor Livesey, on board the ship *Hispaniola*. They are in search of treasure – treasure which was buried on a faraway island by the notorious Captain Flint. Flint may be dead, but he's not forgotten by the pirates who once sailed with him, and who will stop at nothing to find the whereabouts of the lost treasure. Pirates like Blind Pew, Black Dog and the scheming Long John Silver – the most dangerous of them all.

Treasure Island is a true classic, and now this tale of intrigue and excitement has been carefully abridged and beautifully illustrated for younger readers.

Contents

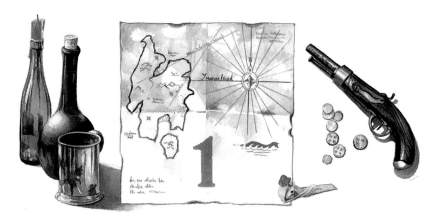

The Old Sea Dog at the Admiral Benbow

SQUIRE TRELAWNEY, Dr. Livesey, and the rest of those gentlemen have asked me to write down all I know about Treasure Island. I take up my pen in the year 17— and go back to the time when my father kept the Admiral Benbow Inn, and the old seaman first took up lodging under our roof.

I remember him as if it were yesterday, as he came plodding to the inn door, his sea chest behind him in a wheelbarrow; a tall, strong, heavy, nut-brown man with his pigtail falling over the shoulders of his soiled, blue coat, and a sabre cut across one cheek. I remember him looking around the cove and whistling to himself as he did so, and then breaking out into that old sea-song that he sang so often afterwards:

> "*Fifteen men on The Dead Man's Chest –*
> *Yo-ho-ho, and a bottle of rum!*"

He rapped on the door and, when my father appeared, called for a glass of rum. When it was brought to him, he drank it slowly, still looking about him at the cliffs and up at our signboard.

"This is a handy cove," he said. "Much company, mate?"

My father said, "No, very little company."

"Then it's the place for me," he said. "Call me Captain." He threw down three or four gold pieces. "Tell me when I've worked through that."

He was a very silent man. Each day he walked around the cove, or up on the cliffs with a brass telescope. Each evening he sat in the parlour next to the fire, and drank rum and water. People left him alone.

Every day when he came back from his stroll, he asked if any seafaring man had passed by. And when a seaman stayed at the Admiral Benbow (as they sometimes did on the way to Bristol) he would look in at him through the curtained door before coming into the parlour. Then one day he promised me a silver fourpenny piece each month if I watched for 'a seafaring man with one leg' and let him know if a man like that appeared.

How that person haunted my dreams! On stormy nights when the winds

shook the four corners of the house, I would see the one-legged man – first with his leg cut off at the knee, then at the hip, then as a monster whose one leg was in the middle of his body! And in the worst of my nightmares, this creature would leap and run after me over hedge and ditch. Altogether, I paid dearly for that monthly fourpenny piece.

But I was less afraid of the captain than others were. There were nights when he became drunk and frightened them with his dreadful stories about hanging, and walking the plank, and storms at sea. He stayed week after week, then month after month. His money was soon used up, but my father was a sick man and too afraid to ask for more.

Dr. Livesey came late one afternoon to see my father. The doctor stopped to eat dinner with my mother, then went into the parlour. He was a neat, pleasantly-mannered man with white hair, quite different from that filthy scarecrow of a pirate sitting with his arms on a table, drunk with rum. Suddenly, the captain began to sing his song:

"Fifteen men on the Dead Man's Chest –
Yo-ho-ho, and a bottle of rum!
Drink and the devil had done for the rest –
Yo-ho-ho, and a bottle of rum!"

Dr. Livesey looked up angrily before he went on talking to old Taylor, the gardener. The captain waved a hand for silence and voices in the room stopped at once – all except Dr. Livesey's.

The captain swore softly. "Silence, there, between decks!"

"Were you addressing me, sir?" said the doctor.

The captain told him he was and swore again.

"I have only one thing to say to you, sir," replied the doctor. "If you keep on drinking rum, the world will soon be rid of a dirty scoundrel!"

The captain sprang to his feet and drew a knife. The doctor didn't move, but spoke calmly, as before.

"If you do not put that knife away this instant," he said, "I promise, upon my honour, you shall hang at the next court session."

Then followed a battle of looks between them, but the captain soon put away his weapon and resumed his seat, grumbling like a beaten dog.

"I'm a magistrate as well as a doctor," Dr. Livesey told him, "and if I hear a complaint about you, I'll have you hunted down and driven away."

Soon after, Dr. Livesey rode off on his horse. But the captain was silent for the rest of that evening, and for many evenings to come.

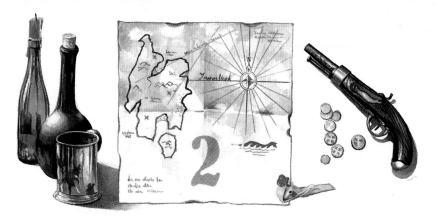

Black Dog Appears and Disappears

IT WAS a bitterly cold winter with hard frosts and heavy gales. My father grew weaker daily and we knew he would not live to see the Spring.

One January morning, when the sun was still low in the sky and the cove white with frost, the captain got up earlier than usual and set off for the beach, his brass telescope under his arm and a cutlass swinging under his coat. Mother was upstairs and I was laying the breakfast table, ready for the captain's return. Suddenly, the parlour door opened and a stranger stepped inside.

He was a pale man with two fingers missing from his left hand. Although he wore a cutlass, he did not look like a fighting man, and he puzzled me. He was not dressed as a sailor, but nevertheless there was a smack of the sea about him. I asked him what he wanted and he said he would take some rum, but before I could fetch it he said, "Is this table for my mate Bill?"

"I don't know your mate Bill," I said. "The breakfast is for the captain."

"My mate Bill would be called the captain," said the stranger, "and he has a cut on one cheek. Now, is he in this house?"

I told him the captain was out walking and the man decided to wait.

When we heard the captain returning, the stranger pulled me behind the parlour door. I was alarmed, but I saw that he, too, looked frightened.

"We'll give Bill a little surprise," he said.

The captain strode in, slamming the door behind him.

"Bill," said the stranger, trying to sound bold.

The captain spun round and saw us. He looked as if he had seen a ghost. "Black Dog!" he gasped.

"Who else? Black Dog, come to see his old shipmate Billy."

"Well, what do you want?" said the captain.

"I'll take a glass of rum from this dear child," said Black Dog. "Then we'll sit down, Billy, and talk like old shipmates."

I fetched the rum and they told me to go away, so I went into the bar. For a long time I could hear nothing, but then the voices grew louder and I could pick up a word or two, mostly oaths, from the captain.

"No, no, no, and that's an end of it!" he cried once. "If it comes to hang-ing, we'll all hang!"

There was the sound of a chair and table going over, then the clash of steel and a cry of pain. Black Dog ran out with blood streaming from his shoulder, chased by the captain. Black Dog, in spite of his wound, quickly disappeared over the edge of the hill while the captain stared after him before turning back to the house.

"Are you hurt?" I asked.

"Rum!" he said. "I must get away from here. Rum, rum!"

I ran to fetch it. Then I heard him fall and hurried back to find him on the parlour floor. My mother came running downstairs to help me and between us we raised his head. His eyes were closed and his breathing was very loud and hard.

It was a happy relief for us when Dr. Livesey arrived to see my father. He took one look at the captain and said, "This man has had a stroke."

Suddenly, the captain opened his eyes. "Where's Black Dog?"

"There's no Black Dog here," said the doctor. "You've been drinking and have had a stroke, as I warned you. Now, I'll help you to your bed."

The Black Spot

ABOUT NOON, I took the captain a cold drink and his medicine. "Jim," he said, "you're the only one here that's worth anything, and you know I've always been good to you. Now, you can see I'm pretty low. You'll bring me some rum, won't you?"

"The doctor – " I began.

He cursed the doctor. "One glass won't hurt me, Jim, and I'll give you a golden guinea for it."

"I don't want your money," I said, "except that which you owe my father. I'll get you one glass, and no more."

When I brought it, he seized it greedily and drank it all.

"Did the doctor say how long I was to lie here?" he asked.

"A week at least," I said.

"Thunder!" he cried. "A week! I can't do that. They'll have the black spot on me by then. They'll get wind of me and come." He had pulled himself up in the bed and was holding my shoulder with a grip that almost made me cry out. Now he fell back and lay silent for a while.

"Jim," he said at last. "You saw that seafaring man today?"

"Black Dog?"

"Ah! Black Dog," he said. "He's a bad one, but there's worse than him. It's my old sea chest they're after, Jim. Now, if they tip me the black spot, you go to that doctor. Tell him to bring the law to the Admiral Benbow. He'll catch Flint's crew, all that's left of 'em. I was Flint's first mate and I'm the only one that knows the place. He gave it to me when he was dying. But do nothing unless they get the black spot on me, or unless you see the seafaring man with one leg, Jim – him above all."

"But what is the black spot, Captain?"

"It's a summons, mate. I'll tell you if they give me that. Keep your eyes open, Jim, and I'll share everything with you equally, upon my honour." His voice grew weaker and at last he fell into a heavy sleep.

That evening, my poor father died quite suddenly, which put all other

matters to one side. I was kept busy with visits from the neighbours, arranging the funeral and carrying on all the work of the inn. I was too busy to worry about the captain.

He got downstairs the next morning and had his meals as usual, although he ate very little and drank more than his normal supply of rum. He helped himself from the bar and no one dared to stop him.

The day after the funeral, at about three o'clock on a foggy, frosty afternoon, I was standing at the door thinking sad thoughts about my father when I saw someone coming along the road. He was blind, for he tapped before him with a stick, and had a green shade over his eyes and nose. He was hunched over and wore a huge, old, tattered sea-cloak with a hood. I never in my life saw a more dreadful-looking figure. He stopped a little way from the house and raised his head.

"Will any kind friend tell a poor blind man where he is?" he said.

"You are at the Admiral Benbow, Black Hill Cove, my good man," I said.

"I hear a young voice," he said. "Will you give me your hand, my kind young friend, and lead me in?"

I held out my hand, and the horrible, soft-spoken, eyeless creature gripped it hard. "Now, boy," he said. "Take me in to the captain or I'll break your arm!" And he gave it a wrench that made me cry out.

I took him into the parlour where our sick, old buccaneer was sitting, dazed with rum. The captain raised his eyes and a look of mortal fear passed over his face.

"Now, Bill, sit where you are," said the blind beggar. "I can't see, but I can hear a finger stirring. Hold out your right hand. Boy, take his right hand by the wrist and bring it near to my right."

We both obeyed, and I saw him pass something into the captain's palm.

"And now that's done," said the blind man. And with incredible nimbleness, he skipped out of the parlour and onto the road. I heard his stick tap-tap-tapping away into the distance.

The captain opened his hand and looked into his palm. "Ten o'clock!" he cried. "Six hours. We'll do them yet." And he sprang to his feet.

But as he did so, he put a hand to his throat, swayed for a moment, then fell with a peculiar sound, face down onto the floor.

I ran to him at once, calling to my mother, but it was too late.

The captain was dead.

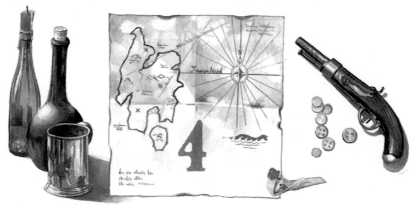

The Sea Chest

I TOLD my mother what I knew and we saw at once that we were in a difficult and dangerous position. Some of the captain's money was due to us, but it was not likely that his shipmates – including Black Dog and the blind beggar – would give up their booty to pay the dead man's debts.

I could not go to Dr. Livesey and leave my mother alone. The neighbourhood seemed to be haunted with approaching footsteps and there were moments when I jumped out of my skin with terror. Finally, we decided to seek help in the nearby village.

It was dark when we reached the village, but we got no help from the villagers. The name of Flint was well known and it filled them with terror. There was no one who would help defend us at the inn.

"Then we'll go back," my mother said. "I'll not lose money that belongs to my boy. We'll have that chest open if we die for it."

Not a man would go with us, but they gave me a loaded pistol then sent a lad to Dr. Livesey's in search of armed help.

A full moon was beginning to rise through the upper edges of the fog as my mother and I made our way back. We slipped noiselessly along beside the hedges until we were inside the Admiral Benbow with the door closed behind us. I slipped the bolt at once and we stood for a moment in the dark, alone in the house with the dead man.

"Draw the blind, Jim," said my mother.

I did so, then went down on my knees beside the body. Close to the captain's hand was a little piece of paper, blackened on one side. I had no doubt this was the *black spot*. On the other side was some writing: *You have till ten tonight.* And as I read it, our old clock struck six.

"The key to the chest, Jim," said my mother.

It was around the captain's neck on a bit of tarry string, which I cut. Then we hurried up to his room.

His box was like any other seaman's chest on the outside, the letter 'B' burned into the top with a hot iron, and the corners smashed and broken by

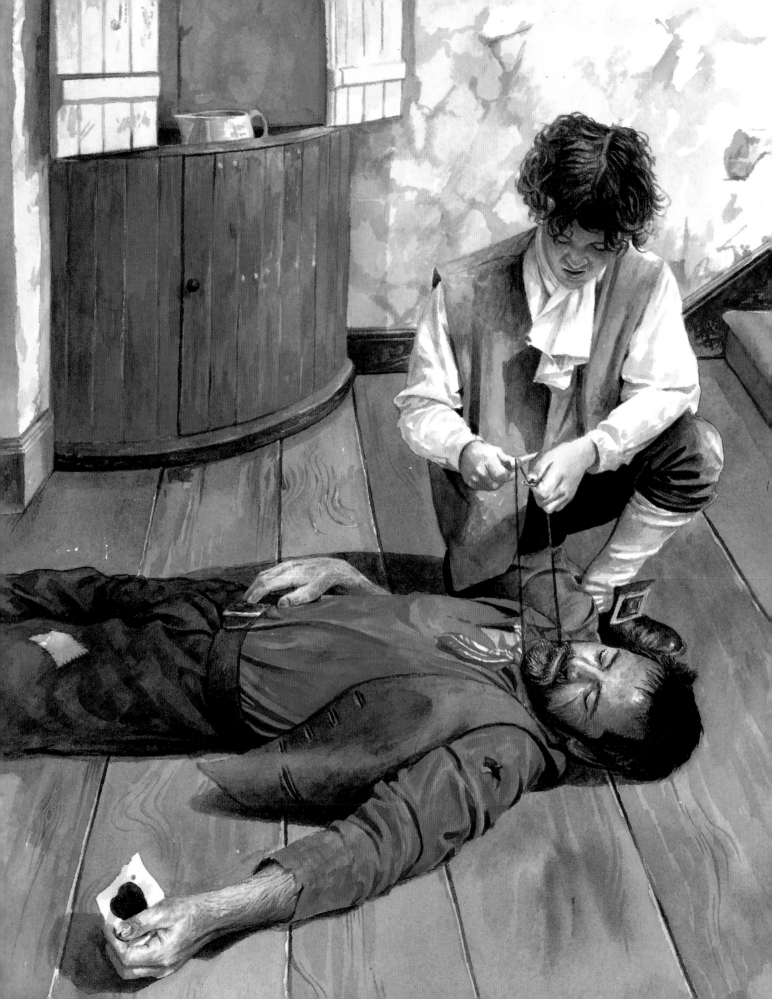

long, rough use. A strong smell of tobacco and tar arose from the inside. A suit of good clothes lay on the top, then several sticks of tobacco, two pistols, a piece of bar silver, an old watch and some other trinkets of little value. Underneath was an old boat-cloak, white with sea-salt. My mother pulled it up impatiently – and there lay a bundle of papers tied up in oilcloth, and a canvas bag that jingled with gold.

"I'll show these rogues that I'm an honest woman," said my mother. "I'll take what's due to me and not a penny more."

There were all kinds of gold coins in the bag – Spanish doubloons, French coins, pieces of eight – but my mother began to count out only the English guineas she needed to settle the captain's debt.

I put my hand on her arm, for I had heard a terrifying sound – the tap-tap-tapping of the blind man's stick upon the road! It came nearer and nearer as we held our breath. Then it struck sharply on the inn door and we heard the handle turning and the bolt rattling. A silence followed, then the tapping started again and slowly died away.

"Mother," I said, "take all the money and let's be going." I was certain the blind man would return with his deadly friends.

But my mother, although frightened, would not take more than was due to her. She knew her rights, she said, and was having them. She was still arguing with me about it when we heard a low whistle a good way off on the hill. That eerie sound was enough for both of us.

"I'll take what I have," she said, jumping to her feet.

"And I'll take this to square the account," I said, picking up the oilskin packet.

We groped our way downstairs, leaving a candle by the empty chest, then ran from the inn. We were not a moment too soon. The fog was lifting, and only a thin veil of mist around the inn door concealed our escape. We heard running footsteps and looked back to see a light from a lantern tossing to and fro as the newcomers drew closer.

"My dear, take the money and run," my mother said suddenly. "I'm going to faint!"

But instead I helped her off the road, down the bank, and under the arch of a little bridge where we could hide.

Seven or eight men ran past us, the man with the lantern in front. Three men ran together, hand in hand, and I saw that the one in the middle was the blind beggar.

"Down with the door!" he cried.

Four or five of them broke down the door of the inn and ran inside, two

others remaining with the blind man. There was a pause, then a shout from the house: "Bill's dead!"

The blind man swore at them. "Search him, some of you! The rest go aloft and get the chest!"

I heard their feet rattle up the stairs, and then the window of the captain's room was thrown open and a man shouted down.

"Pew, they've been before us. Someone's searched the chest."

"Is it there?" roared the blind man Pew.

"The money's there, but Flint's papers have gone."

"It's these people of the inn – it's that boy. I wish I'd put his eyes out!" cried Pew. "Scatter lads, and find them."

I heard furniture being thrown over and doors kicked in; then the men came out onto the road and told Pew we were nowhere to be found. At that moment, two whistles came from the hillside, which I quickly guessed was a signal to warn the pirates of approaching danger.

"That's Dirk," said one. "We'll have to go."

"No, the boy can't be far!" screamed Pew. "Oh, shiver my soul, if only I had eyes!"

Two of the men began to look around half-heartedly, but the others stood uncertainly on the road.

"You could have thousands, you fools, and you stand around!" shouted Pew. "You'd be as rich as kings if you could find it."

"We've got the doubloons!" grumbled one of the others.

"They might have hidden the blessed thing," said another.

Pew became angry and struck at them right and left with his stick, hitting more than one. Suddenly there was the sound of horses and riders, then a pistol shot. The pirates cursed the blind beggar and ran. Pew tried to follow, tapping wildly with his stick.

"Johnny, Black Dog, Dirk!" he cried. "You won't leave old Pew, mates – not old Pew!"

Four or five riders came at full gallop down the slope. Pew turned with a scream – and ran right under the nearest horse! His cry rang high into the night as the horse's hooves trampled over him.

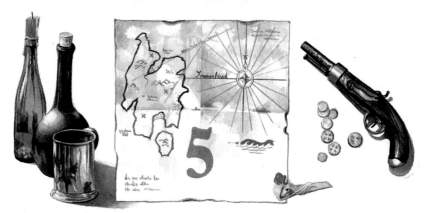

The Map

I LEAPT from the ditch and called out to the riders. One was the boy who had been sent to Dr. Livesey's; the others were revenue officers. News of a pirate ship in the bay had sent them looking, and the boy had met them on his way.

Pew was stone dead, but the other pirates escaped back to their ship in the darkness. By the time the revenue officers reached the bay, the vessel was already setting sail.

We took my mother to a house in the village. Then I went back to the Admiral Benbow with the supervisor of the revenue officers, Mr. Dance. Everything inside the inn had been smashed and broken. We were ruined.

"What were they after, Hawkins?" asked Mr. Dance.

"They got the money from the chest," I said, "but I believe I have the thing they wanted most. It's in my pocket, but I should like to get it to a safe place. I thought perhaps, Dr. Livesey – "

"Quite right," said Mr. Dance. "He's a gentleman and a magistrate. I'll ride with you and report Pew's death."

We rode hard all the way, but Dr. Livesey was not at his house.

"He's at Squire Trelawney's," his maid informed us.

So we rode on to the squire's house. A servant took us into the library where the squire and Dr. Livesey sat on either side of a large fire.

The squire was a tall, broad man with a rough-and-ready look about his red face. "Come in, Mr. Dance," he said.

"Hello, Jim," said the doctor. "What brings you here?"

Mr. Dance told his story and the two men listened with interest.

"And so, Jim," said the doctor, when Mr. Dance had finished, "you have the thing that they were after, have you?"

"Here it is, sir," I said, and gave him the oilskin packet.

The doctor looked at it, then put it into his coat pocket. "Squire," he said, "when Dance has had his ale, he must be off on His Majesty's service. But I want young Hawkins to sleep at my house, so I propose we give him some supper."

So a big pigeon pie was brought in and I ate a hearty meal.

"Now, Squire," said Dr. Livesey, "you've heard of this Flint, I suppose?"

"Heard of him!" cried the squire. "He was the blood-thirstiest pirate that sailed the seas."

"Well, I've heard of him myself," said the doctor. "But the point is, did he have money?"

"Money! What else were those villains after but money?"

"Then suppose I had in my pocket some clue to where Flint buried his treasure," said the doctor. "Would that treasure amount to much?"

"If you have the clue you talk about, sir," said the squire, "I'll fit out a ship in Bristol dock, take you and Hawkins with me, and have that treasure if I have to search for a year!"

We opened the packet and found two things – a book and a sealed paper. The book listed the names of the ships Flint had plundered and the amounts of money taken. The paper was a map of an island. The island was about nine miles long and five across, with two harbours. There was a hill in the centre marked *The Spyglass*, and three crosses in red ink, two on the north side of the island, one in the south-west. Beside the one in the south-west were the words: *Bulk of treasure here.* On the back of the map, the same person had written:

Tall tree, Spyglass shoulder, bearing a point to the N of NNE.
Skeleton Island ESE and by E.
Ten feet.
The bar silver is in the north cache; you can find it by the east hummock, ten fathoms south of the black crag with the face on it.
The arms are easily found, in the sand hill, N point of north inlet cape, bearing E and a quarter N.

J.F.

Although I was unable to understand any of it, the squire and Dr. Livesey were delighted.

"Tomorrow I start for Bristol," said the squire. "In three weeks we'll have the best ship and the choicest crew in England, sir. Hawkins shall come as cabin boy and you, Livesey, are the ship's doctor. I am admiral. We'll take Redruth, Joyce and Hunter. We'll have favourable winds, a quick passage, and no trouble finding the treasure!"

"Trelawney," said the doctor, "I'll go with you, and so will Jim, I'm sure. There's only one man I'm afraid of."

"And who's that?" cried the squire. "Name the dog, sir!"

"You," replied the doctor, "for you cannot hold your tongue. We aren't the

only men who knew of this paper. Those who attacked the inn tonight want to find the same treasure. None of us must be alone until we get to sea. Jim and I will stick together while you take Joyce and Hunter to Bristol. Not one of us must breathe a word of what we've found."

"Livesey," said the squire, "you are always right. I'll be as silent as the grave."

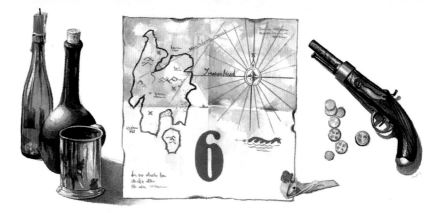

I Go to Bristol

IT WAS longer than the squire imagined before we were ready for the sea. Dr. Livesey had to go to London to find another doctor to look after his practice, and I waited at his home with old Redruth, the gamekeeper. The weeks passed, until one fine day a letter arrived, addressed to Dr. Livesey or 'to be opened in his absence by Jim Hawkins':

Old Anchor Inn, Bristol
MARCH 1, 17 —

Dear Livesey,

As I do not know whether you are at home or still in London, I send copies of this letter to both places.

The ship is bought and fitted, and she lies at anchor, ready for sea. Her name is Hispaniola *and you can't imagine a sweeter schooner.*

I got her through my old friend Blandly who worked hard to find me a suitable ship, as did everyone in Bristol, when they heard the reason for our voyage — treasure, I mean.

"Dr. Livesey won't like that," I said to Redruth. "The squire has been talking, after all." And I read on:

It was the crew that troubled me. I wanted twenty men but could find only six until, quite by accident, I met an old sailor who kept a public house, and who knew all the seafaring men in Bristol. He had lost his health ashore and wanted work as a cook to get to sea again.

I felt sorry for him and, out of pity, engaged him on the spot to be the ship's cook. Long John Silver he is called, and has lost a leg fighting for his country. Well, sir, I thought I had found only a cook, but it was a crew I had discovered. Between Silver and myself we got together a crew of the toughest old salts imaginable — not pretty to look at but fellows of spirit. We could fight a frigate! Long John even got rid of two out of the six I had already engaged, after persuading me of just how unsuitable they would be on such an important adventure.

I am in the most magnificent health, but I shall not enjoy a moment until we set sail. So hurry, Livesey, do not lose an hour. Let young Hawkins go at once to see his mother, and then come full speed to Bristol with Redruth.

John Trelawney

PS: Blandly has found us an admirable fellow to be sailing master, and Long John Silver unearthed a very competent man for a mate, a man named Arrow.

Next morning, Redruth and I set out for the Admiral Benbow where I said goodbye to my mother and to the cove where I had lived since I was born. My mother was in good spirits, but I was still sad to be leaving her for so many months.

The following morning, we went on by coach to Bristol.

Squire Trelawney was living at an inn near the docks. He came out to meet us, dressed like a sea-officer and with a smile on his face.

"Here you are!" he cried. "And the doctor came from London last night. Bravo! The ship's company is complete!"

"When do we sail?" I asked.

"We sail tomorrow!" he said.

After breakfast, the squire gave me a note addressed to Long John Silver. He told me to look for a tavern with a large brass telescope for a sign, and I set off along the busy dock.

The Spyglass tavern was a bright little place with a newly painted sign and red curtains at the windows. The customers were mostly seafaring men, and they talked so loudly that I waited at the door, almost afraid to enter. A man came out of a side room and I knew at a glance that he must be Long John. His left leg was missing, and under his left shoulder he carried a crutch on which he hopped about like a bird.

From the very first mention of Long John in Squire Trelawney's letter, I had been afraid that he might prove to be the one-legged sailor whom I had watched for at the Admiral Benbow. But one look at the man in front of me was enough. I had seen the captain and Black Dog and the blind man Pew, and I thought I knew what a pirate was like – a very different creature, I thought, from this clean and pleasant landlord.

"Mr Silver, sir?" I asked, holding out the note.

"Yes, my lad," he said. "And who may you be?" Then he saw the squire's letter and seemed a little startled. "Oh!" he said in a loud voice. "You are our new cabin boy. I'm pleased to see you." And he took my hand in his large, firm grasp.

Just then, one of the customers at the far side rose and made for the door. I recognised him at a glance. It was the pale-faced man with the missing fingers who had come to the Admiral Benbow!

"Stop him!" I cried. "It's Black Dog!"

"I don't care who he is," cried Silver, "he hasn't paid for his ale. Catch him, Harry!"

One of the men near the door leapt up and ran after Black Dog.

"Who did you say he was?" asked Silver. "Black what?"

"Dog, sir," said I. "Hasn't Squire Trelawney told you of the buccaneers? He was one of them."

"Was he?" said Silver. "Let's see – Black Dog? No, I don't know the name, yet I think I've seen him before. He used to come here with a blind beggar."

"I knew that blind man, too," I said. "His name was Pew."

"It was!" cried Silver.

My suspicions had been reawakened when I saw Black Dog, and I was watching Silver carefully. But he was too deep and too clever for me. When the other man came back without the pirate, Silver scolded him. Then he turned to me.

"I'll put on my old cocked hat and step along with you to Squire Trelawney and report this affair," he said. "It's a serious matter."

On our walk back, he talked about the different ships we passed – their rig, tonnage and nationality. Then he told stories of ships and seamen until I was certain he would make the best possible shipmate.

When we reached the inn, the squire and Dr. Livesey were drinking ale together. Long John told the story of Black Dog, adding, "That was how it was, wasn't it, Hawkins?" And I had to agree.

The two gentlemen regretted that Black Dog had escaped but agreed nothing could be done. Long John took up his crutch, ready to leave.

"All hands aboard by four this afternoon," the squire told him.

"Ay, ay, sir," said the cook, and left us to return to his inn.

"Well, Squire," said Dr. Livesey, "I don't usually put much faith in your discoveries, but I must say this, John Silver suits me. Now, take your hat, Hawkins, and we'll go and see this ship!"

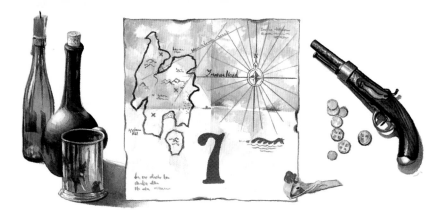

Powder and Arms

THE *HISPANIOLA* lay some way out and we went round the sterns of many others ships to reach her. At last we came alongside and Mr. Arrow, the mate, a weatherbeaten old sailor with earrings in his ears, welcomed us aboard. He and the squire were very friendly, but I soon noticed things were not the same between Squire Trelawney and the captain.

Captain Smollett was a sharp-looking man who seemed angry with everybody on board. He soon told us why. "I'll speak plain," he said. "I don't like this cruise or the men, and I don't like my first officer."

"Perhaps, sir, you don't like the ship?" said the squire, angrily.

"She seems a clever craft," said the captain. "More I can't say."

"Possibly, sir, you don't like your employer either?" said the squire.

Dr. Livesey cut in. "Wait! Such questions only produce ill-feeling." He looked at the captain. "You say you don't like this cruise. Now, why?"

"I was employed on secret orders," said the captain. "Now I find every other man aboard knows more than I do. Do you call that fair?"

"No," said Dr. Livesey, "I don't."

"Next," said the captain, "I hear we're going after treasure – hear it from my own hands, mind you. Now, treasure is ticklish work. I don't like treasure voyages, especially when they're secret."

"You say you don't like the crew," said Dr. Livesey. "Are they not good seamen?"

"I should have been allowed to choose my own men."

"Perhaps you should have," said the doctor. "You don't like Mr. Arrow?"

"He's too friendly with the crew to be a good officer. A mate should keep himself to himself, not drink with the men before the mast!"

"Tell us what you want," said the doctor.

"Very well," said the captain. "The men are putting the powder and arms in the fore-hold. Now, you've a good place under the cabin, why not put them there? Secondly, you are bringing four of your own people with you, and they tell me they are to be berthed forward. Why not give them berths here beside

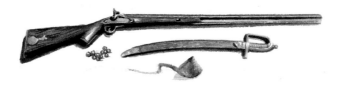

the cabin? Finally, there's been too much blabbing."

"Far too much," agreed the doctor.

"I'll tell you what I've heard. That you have a map of an island, with crosses to show where the treasure is, and that the island lies – " And he named the place exactly.

"I never told that to a soul!" cried the squire.

"The hands knew it, sir," replied the captain. "I don't know who has this map, gentlemen, but it must be kept secret even from me and Mr. Arrow, otherwise I shall ask you to let me resign."

"You wish to keep this matter dark, and you want all the powder and arms near us," said the doctor. "In other words, you fear a mutiny."

"Don't put words into my mouth, sir," said Captain Smollett. "No captain could put to sea if he had proof of that."

And with that he left us.

We went up on deck a little later, and the men were moving the arms and powder when Long John came aboard. He climbed up the side like a monkey and asked them what they were doing.

"My orders!" said the captain, shortly. "You may go below, my man. The crew will want supper."

"Ay, ay, sir," answered the cook, and disappeared at once in the direction of the galley.

"That's a good man, Captain," said the doctor.

"Very likely, sir," replied Captain Smollett. Then he turned to me. "Ship's boy, off with you to the cook and get some work." And as I was hurrying off, I heard him say loudly to the doctor, "I'll have no favourites on my ship."

Like the squire, I hated the captain deeply.

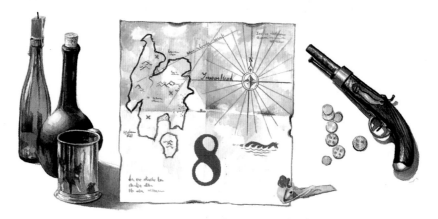

The Apple Barrel

ALL NIGHT, we were getting things stowed in their place, and boatfuls of the squire's friends came to wish him a good voyage and safe return. I was tired when, a little before dawn, the crew began to man the capstan-bars to lift the anchor and one of them cried, "Let's have a song!"

"Ay, ay, mates," said Long John, who was standing by with his crutch under his arm. And he began to sing that song I knew so well:

"Fifteen men on The Dead Man's Chest —"

And the crew joined in the chorus:

"Yo-ho-ho, and a bottle of rum!"

And I remembered the Admiral Benbow and seemed to hear the voice of the captain singing with them. But then the anchor was up and the land and other ships were flitting by on either side. The *Hispaniola* had begun her voyage to the Isle of Treasure.

I will not describe the voyage in detail. The ship proved to be a good ship, the crew were capable seamen, and the captain knew his business. But Mr. Arrow turned out worse than the captain had feared. He could not command the men and began to appear on deck the worse for drink. We could never make out where he got it, but nobody was surprised nor very sorry when, one dark night, he disappeared and was seen no more.

"Overboard!" said the captain. "That saves me putting him in irons."

We were now without a mate but Squire Trelawney had been to sea, and his knowledge made him useful. And the coxwain, Israel Hands, was an experienced seaman. He was a great friend of Long John Silver.

All the crew respected and even obeyed Silver. He was kind to me, and always pleased to see me in the galley, which he kept as clean as a new pin. He kept his parrot in a cage in one corner.

"I call my parrot Captain Flint," he told me, "after the famous buccaneer."

And the parrot would say, "Pieces of eight! Pieces of eight! Pieces of

eight!" until Silver threw his handkerchief over the cage.

Meanwhile, the squire and Captain Smollett were still on bad terms, and the squire did not try to hide it. The captain only spoke when he was spoken to, but confessed that he liked the ship and that he seemed to have been wrong about the crew, who had all behaved fairly well.

Every man on board seemed happy, and so they should have been for there was never a ship's company so well looked after, with double rations of rum, plenty of food to eat, and always a barrel of apples for any man to help himself.

And it was the apple barrel that saved all our lives.

It was about the last day of our outward voyage, and we expected to see Treasure Island before the following noon. There was a steady breeze and the *Hispaniola* rolled gently in a quiet sea. Just after sundown, when all my work was done, I thought I'd like an apple, so I went on deck. The barrel was almost empty, so I climbed right inside and sat down. There, in the dark with the rocking movement of the ship, I nearly fell asleep.

Suddenly, the barrel shook as a heavy man sat down and leaned against it. I was about to jump up when he began to speak. It was Silver. And before I had heard a dozen words, I understood that the lives of all the honest men aboard depended on me alone!

"Flint was cap'n, not I," said Silver. "I was quartermaster. In the same battle that I lost my leg, Pew lost his sight."

"Ah, Flint was the flower of the flock!" said the voice of the youngest hand.

"I got two thousand when I sailed with Flint," said Silver. "Not bad for a man before the mast, and now it's safe in a bank. Gentlemen of fortune live rough and they risk hanging, but they eat and drink well and, when a cruise is over, it's hundreds of pounds not hundreds of farthings in their pockets. When I'm back from this cruise, I'll live like a gentleman! Not before time, you say. Ah, but I've lived easy in the past, except when at sea. How did I begin? Before the mast, like you!"

"I'll tell you now," said the lad, "I didn't like the job till I had this talk with you, John, but I'm with you now. Here's my hand on it."

"A brave lad, and smart, too," said Silver, and they shook hands so heartily that the barrel rocked.

By this time, I understood what was happening. A 'gentleman of fortune' was no more than a common pirate, and Silver had just turned an honest seaman into one – perhaps the last honest man left aboard!

Silver gave a little whistle and a third man joined them.

"Dick's with us," said Silver.

"Oh, I knew Dick was all right," replied the voice of the coxwain, Israel Hands. "He's no fool, is Dick. But, look here, when are we going to make our move? I've had enough o' Cap'n Smollett, by thunder!"

"The last moment, that's when," said Silver. "Listen, Smollett's a first-class seaman, and can sail the ship for us. The squire and the doctor have a map – I don't know where, do you? No? Well then, they can find the stuff for us and help get it aboard, then we'll see. If I was sure of you all, I'd have Cap'n Smollett navigate us half-way home before I struck. But I know the sort you are, so I'll finish 'em at the island, as soon as the stuff's on board."

"What will we do with them?" asked Dick.

"My vote is they should die," said Silver. "I don't want 'em coming home to tell their tales. Now, Dick, I'm thirsty, so get me an apple."

You can imagine the terror I was in! I would have leapt out and ran if I could have found the strength, but my limbs would not move. I heard Dick begin to rise, then Hands said: "Let's have rum, John."

So Dick went to fetch rum instead, and I heard Hands say, "Not another man will join," to Silver, so I knew that at least there were still some honest men aboard.

I looked up and saw the moon had risen. At the same time, the voice of the lookout shouted, "Land-ho!"

There was a great rush of feet across the deck. I quickly slipped out of the barrel and ran towards the stern of the ship, coming out on the open deck in time to join Hunter and Dr. Livesey.

A belt of fog had lifted and, away to the south-west, we saw two hills about a couple of miles apart. Rising behind one of them was a third and higher hill, its peak still buried in fog. I heard Captain Smollett issuing orders, and the *Hispaniola* was turned so that it would just clear the island on the east.

"Has any man seen that island before?" he asked.

"I have, sir," said Silver. "I was cook on a trading ship that stopped to take on water there. A safe place to anchor is on the south side, behind a little island they call Skeleton Island. The three hills we can see run south, and the big one is called Spyglass."

"I've a chart here," said Captain Smollett. "See if it's the place."

Long John looked excited as he took the paper, but he was to be disappointed. It was not the map we found in the chest, but a copy – without names and heights, only the red crosses and written notes.

Silver hid his disappointment. "Yes, sir. This is the spot, and very prettily drawn it is. Who might have done that, I wonder?"

"I'll ask you later to give us some help," said the captain. "You may go now."

Silver moved next to me. "This island's a sweet spot for a lad to go ashore," he said. "When you want to do a bit of exploring, you just ask old John." And he clapped me on the shoulder in a friendly way.

Dr. Livesey called me to him. He had left his pipe below and was about to ask me to fetch it, but I spoke quickly. "Doctor, get the captain and squire down to the cabin. I have terrible news."

He went across to the other two and spoke briefly, and they all went below. Not long after, a message came that I was wanted in the cabin.

I found them seated round the table, a bottle of Spanish wine and some raisins before them.

"Now, Hawkins," said the squire. "What is it you have to say?"

I told them quickly what Silver and the others had said. They listened without interruption, their eyes never leaving my face.

"You were right and I was wrong, captain," the squire said when I had finished. "I was a fool, but now I await your orders."

"No more a fool than I," said the captain. "I never knew a mutinous crew that didn't show signs of it before, but this crew beats me."

"That's Silver," said the doctor. "He's a remarkable man."

"He'd look remarkably well hanging from a yard-arm, sir!" replied the captain. "We can't turn back or they would know at once, but we have time – at least until this treasure is found. Your men are honest, squire?"

"As honest as myself," declared Trelawney.

"Three," said the captain, "and ourselves make seven, counting Hawkins here. Now, about the honest hands."

"Most likely the men Trelawney chose before he met Silver," said the doctor.

"No," said the squire. "Hands was one of them."

"Well, gentlemen," said the captain, "we must wait and watch."

I began to feel desperate. There were only seven out of the twenty-six we could rely on, and out of these seven, I was a boy. So the grown men on our side were just six to their nineteen!

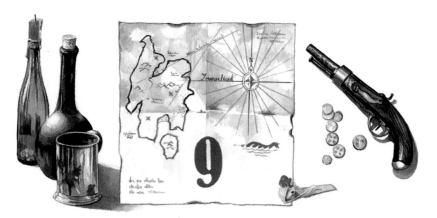

My Shore Adventure

WE COVERED a good distance during the night and, when I came up on deck the next morning, we were lying about half a mile to the south-east of the island. Grey-coloured woods covered a large part of the surface, broken by streaks of yellow sand and high, rocky hills. All these were strangely shaped, and Spyglass Hill was three or four hundred feet taller than the rest.

The *Hispaniola* was rolling in the ocean swell and I felt a little sick standing there with an empty stomach. Perhaps it was this, or perhaps it was the grey, melancholy look of the island, for although the sun shone bright and hot and the shore birds were flying all around us, my heart sank to my boots. From that first look onwards, I hated the very thought of Treasure Island.

There was no wind, and the boats had to be got out to pull us three or four miles round the island to the safe anchorage behind Skeleton Island. I went in one of the boats.

The heat was fierce and the men grumbled over their work, but they became truly threatening when they came back aboard. They lay about on the deck, growling together, and every order was received with a black look.

"If I risk another order," said the captain, "they'll mutiny. There's only one man who can help us."

"And who is that?" asked the squire.

"Silver, sir. He is as anxious as you and I to keep things calm. Let's allow them an afternoon ashore. If they all go, we'll have the ship and we can defend it against them. If some go, mark my words, Silver will bring them back as gentle as lambs."

Loaded pistols were given to all the men we could be sure of, and Hunter, Joyce and Redruth were told what was happening. Then the captain went on deck and spoke to the crew.

"Lads, we've had a hot day, and all are tired. The boats are still in the water, and any man who wants to can go ashore for the afternoon. I'll fire a gun half an hour before sundown to call you back."

I think the silly fellows thought they would fall over the treasure as soon as they landed, for they all stopped sulking. Silver arranged things, and eventually six men stayed aboard and the others, with Silver, got into the boats.

It was then that I had the first of the mad ideas that helped so much to save our lives. If six men were left it was plain we could not take control of the ship; and because only six were left, our party did not need my immediate help. So I decided to go on shore, and quickly slipped over the side into the nearest boat.

"Is that you, Jim?" said one of the rowers. "Keep your head down." Silver called from another boat, wanting to know if it was me, and from that moment on I began to regret what I had done.

The crews raced for the beach, but the boat I was in reached the shore first. I swung myself out and plunged into the nearest thicket of trees while Silver and the rest were still a hundred yards behind.

"Jim! Jim!" I heard him shouting, but I ran on until I could run no longer.

I crossed marshy ground and came out on an open sandy piece of land about a mile long, dotted with trees. For the first time, I felt free to explore, and I turned this way and that between the trees. There were flowering plants that I had never seen before, and once I saw a snake raise its head from a rock and hiss at me!

Then I came to some trees whose branches hung thick and low along the sand. The marsh was steaming in the strong sun, and the outline of Spyglass Hill trembled through the haze.

All at once, I heard a bustling noise and the sound of men's voices. I crawled under cover of the nearest tree, then raised my head and looked through the leaves. There, in a little dell beside the marsh, Long John Silver and another member of the crew stood talking together.

"Tom," Silver was saying, "it's because I want to save your neck that I'm a-warning you!"

"Silver," said the other man, "you're old and you're honest, or have the name for it, and you've money, too. And you're brave, or I'm mistaken. But you tell me you'll let yourself be led away with those swabs? Not you! And I'd sooner die than that turn against my duty – "

There was a sudden noise: a long, horrible scream echoed around the rocks of Spyglass Hill and sent a hundred marsh birds flying. I had found one honest man here, and that terrible scream told me of another.

"John!" cried Tom. "What in heaven's name was that?"

"That?" replied Silver, with eyes that gleamed like glass splinters. "I reckon that'll be Alan."

"Alan!" cried Tom, angrily. "Then rest his soul for a true seaman! And as

for you, John Silver, you're a mate of mine no more. You've killed Alan, have you? Kill me too, if you can!"

And the brave fellow turned his back on the cook and set off back to the beach. But he did not get far. With a cry, Silver whipped the crutch from under his arm and sent it hurtling through the air. It struck poor Tom violently between the shoulders and, with a gasp, he fell. Silver, quick as a monkey, was on top of him, and twice buried his knife up to the hilt in that poor body.

For the next few moments, the whole world seemed to swim before me in a whirling mist. When I was myself again, the monster had his crutch under his arm and was cleaning his blood-stained knife on a wisp of grass.

As speedily and silently as I could manage, I crawled away to the open part of the wood, and as soon as I was clear of the thicket, I ran as I'd never run before.

The Man of the Island

I WAS close to the foot of a little hill when a new danger brought me to a standstill. The hill was steep and stony, and gravel fell rattling and jumping between the trees. I looked up and saw a figure leap behind a tree. I could not tell whether it was a bear, man or monkey but did not wait to find out. I turned on my heel and headed back towards the boats.

The figure appeared again and moved with the speed of an animal, but I knew now that it was a man. I remembered I had a pistol and this gave me courage to turn back towards him. He stepped out to meet me.

"Who are you?" I asked.

"Ben Gunn," he answered. "Poor Ben Gunn, who hasn't spoken to a soul these three years." His skin was burnt by the sun and his clothes were rags and tatters of old ship's canvas. Around his waist he wore a brass-buckled belt.

"Three years!" I cried. "Were you shipwrecked?"

"No, mate," he said. "Marooned."

I had heard the word before. It meant a horrible punishment, common among pirates, in which an offender is left behind on some desolate and distant island with just a little powder and shot.

"I've lived on wild goats and berries and oysters," he continued. "You don't happen to have a piece of cheese, do you? Many's the long night I've dreamed of cheese."

"If I ever get on board again," I said, "you shall have as much cheese as you want."

"Who'll stop you?" he said. "And what do you call yourself?"

"Jim," I told him.

"Well, Jim," he said, lowering his voice to a whisper. "I'm rich. Rich, I say! Now tell me, that ain't Flint's ship, is it?"

I began to feel I had found a friend, and I answered him at once. "No, Flint is dead, but there are some of Flint's men aboard."

"Not a man – with one – leg?" he gasped.

"Silver?" I asked.

"Ay, Silver!" he said. "That was his name."

"He's the cook, and the ringleader, too." And I told him the whole story of our voyage, and the danger we were in.

When I had finished, he patted me on the head. "You're a good lad, Jim, but you're all in trouble, ain't you? Well, you just trust Ben Gunn. Would your squire be generous if I helped you all, do you think? Generous to the tune of – say – a thousand pounds, out of money that's really mine?"

"I'm sure he would," I said.

"*And* give me a passage home?"

"The squire's a gentleman," I told him. "Besides, if we got rid of the others, we'd want you to help work the ship home."

"So you would," he said, and seemed relieved. "I was in Flint's ship when he and six seamen buried the treasure. They were ashore a week, then Flint returned alone in a little boat. He had murdered the others, although not a man aboard could work out how he had done it. Then, three years back, I was in another ship when we sighted this island. 'Boys,' I said. 'Here's Flint's treasure. Let's go ashore and find it.' Twelve days we looked for it, and every day they got angrier with me, until one morning they went back to the ship. 'Ben Gunn,' says they, 'here's a musket, a spade and a pick-axe. Stay here and find Flint's money for yourself.' Well, Jim, three years I've been here now, and not a proper bite of food from that day to this." He winked at me. "Now go and tell your squire that Ben Gunn is a good man."

"But how do I get on board?" I asked.

"There's a boat I made which I keep under the white rock. If worse comes to the worst, we'll use that after dark."

Just then, with still an hour to go before sundown, the whole island echoed to the thunder of a cannon.

"They've begun to fight!" I cried. "Follow me!"

I began to run towards the bay, my terrors all forgotten. Ben Gunn trotted close by my side.

"Left," he said. "Keep to your left, Jim! Under the trees!"

The cannon shot was followed, after some time, by a number of shots from smaller weapons.

Another pause, then not quarter of a mile in front of me, I saw the Union Jack flutter in the air above the wood.

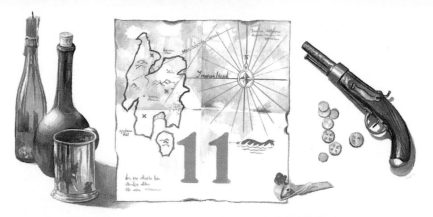

How the Ship was Abandoned

IT WAS about half-past one when the two boats went ashore from the *Hispaniola*. The captain, the squire and I were talking matters over in the cabin. If there had been a breath of wind we should have attacked the six pirates aboard and set sail, but there was no wind. Then Hunter told us that Jim Hawkins had gone ashore with the others.

We never doubted Jim, but we were alarmed for his safety. Would we see him again? We ran on deck. The six scoundrels sat grumbling under a sail; ashore we could see the boats tied up and a man sitting in each.

It was decided that Hunter and I should go ashore with the jolly-boat to see what was happening. We rowed in the direction of the stockade which was mentioned on the map. The two who were left guarding the boats saw us coming and immediately began to discuss what they should do. Had they gone and told Silver, all might have turned out differently, but they had their orders and stayed where they were.

After landing, I jumped out and had not gone more than a hundred yards when I came to the stockade. There, on a hill which had a spring of water almost at the top, stood a strong log-house, fit to hold forty people and with holes for guns on every side. Around this was a wide space, then a fence six feet high, without door or opening and too strong to pull down easily or quickly, and too open to give shelter to attackers.

What particularly pleased me was the spring. Though we had plenty of arms and ammunition and things to eat aboard the *Hispaniola*, we had no water. I was thinking this over when I suddenly heard the terrible cry of a man about to die. 'Jim Hawkins is gone!' was my first thought.

I ran down to the shore and Hunter rowed swiftly back to the ship.

They were all shaken, and Trelawney was white as a sheet. Then I saw that Abraham Gray, one of the hands, was no better.

"There's a man," said Captain Smollett, "who came near to fainting when he heard that cry, Doctor. He might be persuaded to join us."

I told my plan to the captain, and between us we settled the details of how to carry it out. We put Redruth between the cabin and the forecastle, with three or four loaded muskets. Hunter brought the little boat round under the cabin window and Joyce and I loaded her with powder, muskets, bags of biscuits, a cask of brandy and my medicine chest. In the meantime, the squire and the captain stayed on deck and managed to surprise Israel Hands and the other men.

"If any one of you six move or make a signal, that man is dead," said the captain, pointing his guns. The squire did the same.

By this time, we had the boat loaded as much as we dared. Joyce and I got in it with Hunter and made for the shore again, as fast as oars could take us. We touched land in the same place as before, then carried the provisions up to the house inside the stockade. Then, leaving Joyce to guard them, Hunter and I rowed back to the ship and loaded up again. After the second trip, I left Hunter with Joyce and rowed back alone.

The squire was waiting and we loaded the boat for the last time. We took a musket and a cutlass apiece for the squire, myself, Redruth and the captain. The rest of the arms and powder we dropped overboard.

"Abraham Gray!" said Captain Smollett. "I am leaving the ship and order you to follow your captain. I know you are a good man at heart."

There was a scuffle as Gray broke away from the others, a knife-cut on one cheek. "I'm with you, sir," he said.

And the next moment he and the captain had dropped into the boat and we had pushed off from the ship.

But this last trip was different. The boat was badly overloaded, and we had forgotten the ship's cannon until the captain remembered it.

"The gun!" he said.

We looked back to the ship to see the men getting it ready to fire.

"Israel Hands was Flint's gunner," said Gray.

Trelawney, who was the best shot, tried to shoot Hands, but killed another man instead. A cry came from the shore and I turned to see pirates running from the trees towards their boats.

We were halfway to the island when the ship's cannon was fired. The ball missed us but fell into the water near our stern and the waves from it toppled our boat into the sea. Most of the food was lost and we had only two dry guns, but we managed to wade ashore before being cut off by the pirate boats from the island.

We raced to the stockade as the voices of the buccaneers came closer. I guessed there would be a fight and checked my gun.

"Captain," I said, "Trelawney is the best shot, give him your gun. His own is useless."

They exchanged guns and we ran on to the edge of the wood and saw the stockade in front of us. At the same moment, seven pirates appeared at the south-west corner. The squire and I fired, as did Hunter and Joyce from the log-house, and one of the enemy fell whilst the others plunged back into the trees. The fallen man was dead, but as we reloaded our weapons, another shot came from the trees and poor Tom Redruth stumbled and fell. We were able to carry him, groaning and bleeding, into the log-house, but I saw that he would not live long.

The captain checked our stores. "It's a pity we lost the second load of food. We've enough powder and shot, but we're short of rations."

All through the evening the pirates kept thundering away. Shot after shot flew over us, or fell short of the house, kicking up the sand inside the fence. Later, a shout came from the land side:

"Doctor! Squire! Captain!" came the cry.

And I ran to the door in time to see Jim Hawkins, safe and sound, climbing over the stockade.

Inside the Stockade

JIM HAWKINS CONTINUES HIS STORY

AS SOON as Ben Gunn saw the flag, he caught my arm and said, "There's your friends, sure enough."

"Far more likely to be the mutineers," I answered.

"Silver would fly the Jolly Roger flag, if it was," he said. "No, there's been a fight and I reckon your friends have had the best of it. They're ashore in the stockade which Flint built years ago."

"All the more reason I should hurry and join them," I said.

"I won't go there," said Ben, "not until you've seen your gentleman and got his word of honour. When Ben Gunn is wanted, you know where to find him, Jim. And if them pirates camp ashore, they may be sorry for it!"

The ship's cannon was fired and the shot came crashing through the trees, falling less than a hundred yards from where we were standing. The next moment, each of us took to his heels in a different direction.

The firing continued for another hour, and I moved from hiding-place to hiding-place. Then, after a long detour to the east, I made my way down to the shore. The sun had just set and the breeze was ruffling the surface of the sea. The tide was far out and the *Hispaniola* still lay where she had anchored, but with the Jolly Roger, the black flag of piracy, flying above her. On the beach, men were breaking up the jolly-boat with axes, and I could see a great fire glowing amongst the trees.

Eventually, I decided to return to the stockade. I was some way down on the low sandy spit of land which was joined to Skeleton Island. As I rose to my feet, I looked along the spit and saw a high, isolated rock, white in colour. Was this the white rock Ben Gunn had spoken about? I wondered. If it was, some day or other when a boat was wanted I should know where to look for one.

I kept under cover of the woods until I reached the stockade where I was warmly welcomed by my friends.

I told them my story and, before we ate supper, we buried poor old Tom Redruth, who had died. After the meal, the three chiefs got together to discuss

our prospects. Our best hope, it was decided, was to kill off the buccaneers one by one until they hauled down their flag or ran away with the *Hispaniola*.

I was dead tired and soon fell asleep, and was only woken by the sound of voices the next morning.

"A white flag of truce!" I heard someone say – then with a cry of surprise, "Silver himself!"

I ran to a hole in the wall and looked out. Sure enough, there were two men just outside the stockade, one of them waving a white cloth, the other – no less a person than Silver himself – standing calmly by.

It was a cold morning, the sky bright and cloudless, but Silver and his companion were standing knee-deep in a low mist.

"Stop, or we fire!" shouted the captain.

"Flag of truce," cried Silver. "It's Cap'n Silver, sir, to come and talk terms."

"*Cap'n* Silver?" said the captain. "Who's he?"

Long John answered. "These poor lads have chosen me cap'n, after you deserted, sir. We're willing to make peace if we can agree terms. All I ask is your word, Cap'n Smollett, to let me out of the stockade safe and sound before a gun is fired."

"My man," said Captain Smollett, "I have no desire to talk to you, but if you want to talk to me, you may come. There will be no tricks."

Silver approached the stockade, threw his crutch over the fence and, with great skill, climbed after it. Then, with some difficulty, he came up the steep hill of soft sand. He was dressed in a blue coat with brass buttons, and a fine laced hat on the back of his head.

"Aren't you going to let me inside?" he said to the captain. "It's a cold morning to be sitting out on the sand."

"If you had chosen to be an honest man, Silver," replied the captain, "you could be in your warm kitchen. You're either my ship's cook or a common pirate. Now, if you've anything to say, then say it."

"Very well, Cap'n Smollett," said Silver, sitting down on the sand. "You were clever, last night, I don't deny it. One of you is pretty handy with a knife, isn't he? But he won't do it twice, by thunder! We'll have a sentry, and we'll drink less rum. If I'd wakened a second sooner, I'd have caught him in the act. Our man wasn't dead when I reached him."

"Well?" said Captain Smollett, as cool as can be.

Silver's words meant nothing to him, although you wouldn't have guessed it from his manner. But I remembered Ben Gunn's last words to me and realised that the wild man of the island had paid a visit to the buccaneers, and that we now had one less enemy to deal with.

"We want that treasure, and we'll have it," said Silver. "You give us the map and stop shooting poor seamen, and we'll offer you a choice. Either you come aboard ship with us when we have the treasure, and we'll put you ashore somewhere safe, or you can stay here with half the stores and I'll speak to the first ship I see and send 'em here to pick you up."

"Is that all?" said Captain Smollett.

"Every last word, by thunder!" answered Silver.

"Now you'll hear me," said the captain. "If you come up one by one unarmed, I'll clap you in irons and take you home to a fair trial in England. You can't find the treasure. You can't sail the ship. You can't fight us – Gray got away from five of you. Those are the last good words you'll get from me. The next time we meet I'll put a bullet in your back! Now, get out of here!"

Silver's eyes burned with rage. "Give me a hand up!" he cried.

"Not I," replied the captain.

"Who'll give me a hand up?" Silver roared.

None of us moved. Cursing, he crawled along the sand to the porch and hauled himself up on to his crutch.

"Before an hour's up, I'll break your old log-house like a rum bottle!" he cried. "And them that die will be the lucky ones!"

As soon as Silver had gone, the captain went round and prepared us for battle.

"Put out that fire," he ordered. "We don't want smoke in our eyes. Doctor, you take the door. Hunter, take the east side; Joyce, the west. Trelawney, you're the best shot, go with Gray and take the north side where the danger is. Hawkins will stand by to load and give a hand."

An hour passed, and the sun climbed high in the sky. Then, without warning, Joyce lifted his musket and fired. The sound had scarcely died away before a volley of shots rang out all around the stockade. Then there was a silence as the smoke cleared away.

Suddenly, a shout came from the woods and a group of pirates came from the trees on the north side and ran straight to the fence, where they climbed like monkeys and swarmed over the top. The squire and Gray fired again and again. Two fell dead and a third man ran back into the trees. Four were inside the stockade.

"Cutlasses, lads! Fight them in the open!" cried the captain.

I snatched a cutlass from the pile and ran out into the sunlight. More mutineers were swarming up the fence. One man, in a red cap and with a cutlass in his mouth, was already at the top. And yet, at that moment, the fight was over and the victory was ours.

Gray had cut down the big boatswain. Another man was shot as he fired into the house and now lay in agony, his pistol still smoking in his hand. A third, the doctor disposed of with one blow. Of the four who had climbed the fence, only one remained unwounded and was clambering out again with the fear of death upon him.

But we had paid a price for victory. Hunter lay injured, and Joyce had been shot dead through the head, whilst the squire was supporting the captain, one as pale as the other.

"The captain's wounded!" cried Squire Trelawney.

My Sea Adventure

THE pirates did not return.

"They've had enough punishment for one day," said the captain.

His wound, although serious, was not dangerous, but Hunter died a few hours later. After dinner, the doctor and the squire sat beside the captain and they talked. Then, a little past noon, the doctor took his hat, pistols and cutlass, put the map into his pocket, and set off briskly throught the trees.

I guessed he was going to see Ben Gunn, and I envied him his walk in the cool shadow of the woods, with the pleasant smell of the pine trees. I was trapped in the hot sun, with blood and dead bodies all around me. Then I had an idea. I would go and find Ben Gunn's boat! It might be useful to know where it was in case it was needed quickly. I knew I would not get permission to leave the stockade, so I filled my pockets with bread, took two pistols and some powder, and slipped away unnoticed.

I made straight for the east coast. It was late afternoon, still warm and sunny, but a cool sea breeze soon reached me. Then, suddenly, there was the sea. I walked along beside the surf, enjoying the air, until I decided I was far enough south. Then, using some thick bushes as cover, I crept up to the ridge of the narrow spit of sand. From there I could see the white rock along the spit where Ben Gunn had said his boat was hidden.

It took a while to reach it, crawling along on my hands and knees, and it was almost dark when I got there. The boat – a coracle – was hidden in the grass; it was a rough, home-made thing of wood and goat-skins. It was very small, even for me.

Having found the boat, I ought to have returned to the stockade, but I sat down and waited, another idea forming in my head. The last of the daylight disappeared and darkness settled over Treasure Island. There was a big fire on the shore where the pirates sat singing and drinking. The only other light came from the *Hispaniola*, out at sea.

I carried the coracle to the water. It was a very safe boat for a person of my size but very difficult to control, turning in every direction except the one I

wanted to go. It was the tide and not my paddling which got me out to the *Hispaniola*.

The ship was no more than a black shape in the darkness to begin with, but then I was alongside her anchor rope. One cut with my knife and the *Hispaniola* would be carried off by the tide, but a taut anchor rope cut suddenly is as dangerous as a kicking horse. My coracle could be knocked clean out of the water. So I took my knife and cut one strand of the rope at a time, until the vessel was held only by two. Then I waited.

The drunken, angry voices of two men came from the cabin. Then I felt the anchor rope grow slack in the water, so I quickly cut through the last strands as the ship drew closer to me. As I pushed my boat away from it, I felt a light cord that was trailing over the stern of the ship.

I grasped it.

Why I did so, I don't know. But once that the cord was in my hands, curiosity got the better of me and I just had to see inside the cabin. I pulled myself in hand over hand and stood up and looked through the window.

Israel Hands and the man in the red cap were locked in a battle, each with a hand on the other's throat. I dropped back into the boat again just as the wind violently swung the *Hispaniola* round, and the coracle with it. The shouting stopped and I heard feet pounding up to the deck. At last the drunkards were aware of what was happening to their ship.

I lay flat in the coracle as it headed out into the open sea, certain I was going to drown. Gradually, weariness took over and I fell asleep in my sea-tossed little boat, dreaming of home and the old Admiral Benbow.

It was daylight when I awoke. I had drifted to the south-west end of Treasure Island, about a quarter of a mile out at sea. The sun was up, yet still hidden by the great bulk of Spyglass hill, which came down almost to the sea in dangerous-looking cliffs. My first thought was to paddle in and land, but when I saw the jagged rocks around the shore I decided to let the tide take me to a safer landing place on the north side of the island.

The waves rose and fell, and I had to stay flat at the bottom of the coracle so as not to disturb the balance and sink it. I did put a paddle over the side from time to time, giving the little boat a shove or two towards land. It was tiring and slow work.

I did not see the *Hispaniola* until she was in front of me, not half a mile away! But something odd was happening. First she turned north, then suddenly westwards again.

"Nobody is steering her!" I cried. "They must still be drunk!"

The *Hispaniola* swung round again, dangerously close to the coracle. I was

on top of one wave when the ship came over the next, towering above me. There was no time to think. The bowsprit was over my head. I pushed the coracle underwater with my feet and, with one hand, caught the jib-boom.

A dull thud told me that the ship had charged down and smashed the coracle. There was no going back now!

The Fight with Israel Hands

ICRAWLED along the bowsprit and tumbled head-first on to the deck. The two men were there. Red-cap was on his back, one arm out-stretched. Israel Hands was propped against the side, his face white. There was dark blood around them on the deck, and I was sure they had killed each other in their drunken fight. But then Israel Hands turned round with a low moan.

"Brandy," he said.

I went quickly down to the cabin and found a bottle with some brandy left in it, then took it back up to Hands. He drank it greedily.

"By thunder, I wanted that!" he said.

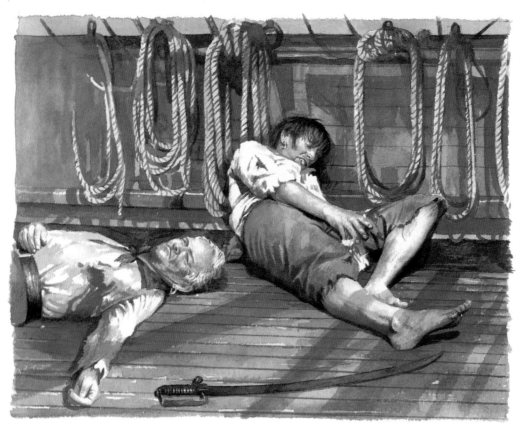

"I've come aboard to take command of this ship, Mr. Hands," I told him. "Please treat me as your captain until further notice." And I immediately took down the Jolly Roger and threw it overboard. "There's an end to Captain Silver!" I said.

He watched me through narrowed eyes. "You'll want to get ashore now, Cap'n Hawkins, but who's to sail the ship? Now, if you give me food and drink, and an old scarf to tie my wound, I'll tell you how to sail her."

"We'll go to the North Inlet and quietly beach her there," I said.

In three minutes I had the *Hispaniola* sailing easily before the wind, along the coast of Treasure Island. Then I lashed the tiller and went below to get a silk handkerchief of my mother's. With my help, Hands bound up the bleeding stab wound in his thigh. He ate a little and had a swallow or two of the brandy, and looked a little better.

The ship skimmed before the breeze like a bird. I began to feel happier about deserting the stockade, but was very aware of the way Hands watched my every move, an odd smile on his face.

We eventually reached the mouth of the North Inlet but dared not beach the ship until the tide allowed, so we ate a silent meal instead.

"Cap'n" said Hands. "S'pose you heave O'Brien's body overboard. I ain't particular as a rule, and I take no blame for killing him, but he ain't a pretty sight, is he?"

"I'm not strong enough," I said. "He stays where he is."

After a moment, he said, "This brandy's too strong. I'd take it kindly, Jim, if you'd step down to the cabin and get me a bottle of wine."

He wanted me to leave the deck, that was plain. But why? I didn't believe the story about the brandy. "White or red?" I asked.

"It's all the same to me, shipmate," he said.

"I'll bring you port," I said, "but I'll have to search for it."

I went below, slipped off my shoes, then went quietly up the other stairs to watch him. He was on his hands and knees and, although his leg obviously hurt him when he moved, he went speedily across to a coil of rope and took a long knife from the centre of it. The blade was smeared with blood, and he tested the point with his hand before slipping the knife under his jacket.

That was all I needed to know. Hands could move about, had a knife and planned to kill me. Yet I was sure he wouldn't make his move until the ship was safely beached. I hurried back to the cabin, picked up a bottle of wine and went up on deck.

He took a good swig from the bottle, saying, "Here's luck!"

The shores of the North Inlet were thickly wooded. We passed the wreck

of a ship that was hung with great webs of seaweed. It was a sad sight, but it showed us the anchorage was calm.

I was so busy with the ship that I forgot to watch Hands carefully. We were nearly on the beach and I was watching the ripples spreading before the bows. Perhaps I heard a creak or saw a shadow moving, or perhaps it was instinct, I don't know. But when I looked round, there was Hands half-way towards me, the knife in his right hand!

Our eyes met and we both cried out. At the same instant, he threw himself forward and I leapt sideways. As I did so, I let go of the tiller. It struck Hands across the chest and stopped him. I snatched a pistol from my belt and pulled the trigger – but it did not fire! The powder was wet with sea-water and I cursed myself for being so careless.

Suddenly, the *Hispaniola* hit the sand and lurched to one side until the deck was at an angle of forty-five degrees. We were both thrown down but I was first on my feet. I climbed up into the sails, and Israel Hands watched me, his mouth wide open with surprise.

Once in a safe place, I reloaded both my pistols. Hands hesitated for a moment, then hauled himself up among the sails, the knife between his teeth. Slowly and painfully, he began to climb.

"One more step, Mr. Hands," I said, "and I'll blow your brains out!"

He stopped. "Jim," he said, taking the dagger from his mouth to speak. "I reckon we'll have to make peace."

Suddenly, his right hand went back over his shoulder and something sang like an arrow through the air! I felt a blow, then a sharp pain, and I was pinned to the mast by my shoulder. In the awful pain and surprise of the moment, both my pistols went off and fell from my hands.

They did not fall alone. With a choked cry, Hands lost his grip on the sails and plunged head first into the water. He surfaced once amongst foam and blood, then sank again for good.

I felt sick and faint. Warm blood ran over my back and chest. The dagger which pinned my shoulder burned like hot iron. But the knife had almost missed and only held me by a pinch of skin. I was shaking and shuddering so badly that this tore away, leaving me tacked to the mast by just my shirt and coat. I ripped myself free and climbed back down.

I did what I could for my wound. It was neither deep nor dangerous, although it bled a good deal. A light evening breeze was blowing as I set about lowering the sails, and by the time I had finished the sun had dropped below the horizon. I then lowered myself over the side into the water, now only waist-deep, and waded ashore.

All I wanted to do now was get back to the stockade. Perhaps I would be blamed a little for running out on them, but I was sure even Captain Smollett would be pleased to learn I had re-taken the *Hispaniola*.

The moon climbed higher in the sky, and at last I came to the borders of the clearing. The log-house itself lay in black shadow, and on the other side a large fire had almost burned itself out. Not a soul stirred, and there were no sounds except that of the breeze.

I moved quickly round to the eastern side, keeping in the shadows. As I got to the corner of the house, I heard a sound that brought joy to my heart — my friends snoring in their sleep! I looked inside, but it was dark and I could see nothing. With my arms in front of me, I walked in.

Suddenly, a voice screamed in the darkness: "Pieces of eight! Pieces of eight! Pieces of eight!"

It was Silver's parrot, Captain Flint!

The sleepers awoke and jumped up.

"Who's there?" a voice cried. It was Silver.

I turned to run, struck violently against one person, then ran into the arms of another. They closed tightly around me.

In the Enemy's Camp

"**B**RING a light, Dick," said Silver.

When it was lit, I saw that five pirates were on their feet, still only half awake from a drunken sleep. A sixth was lying down with a blood-stained bandage around his head.

"So," said Silver, "here's Jim Hawkins, shiver my timbers! It's friendly of you to visit us, Jim."

"Why are you here, and where are my friends?" I demanded.

Silver replied smoothly. "Yesterday morning, Dr. Livesey came down with a flag of truce. 'Cap'n Silver,' says he, 'you're beaten. The ship's gone.' We looked out and, by thunder, the ship *had* gone! 'Well, let's bargain,' says the doctor. So we bargained, he and I, and here we are: stores, brandy, log-house, everything. As for your friends, they've walked off and I don't know where they are. 'How many are you?' I asks the doctor. 'Four,' says he, 'and one of us wounded. As for that boy, I don't know where he is and I don't much care.' Those were his last words to me."

"Now I've got a thing or two to tell you," I said. "You're in a bad way – ship lost, treasure lost, men lost, your whole plan a wreck. And if you want to know who did it – it was me! I was in the apple barrel and heard all that you said. And as for the *Hispaniola*, it was I who cut her anchor rope and killed the men you left aboard her. And it's me who has sailed her to a place where you'll not find her. Kill me if you please, but if you spare me I'll do what I can to save you from the gallows."

"Kill him!" shouted one of the men. He sprang forward with a knife.

"Get back there!" cried Silver. "Maybe you thought you were cap'n here, Tom Morgan, but cross me and I'll feed you to the fishes!"

"But Tom's right," said one of the others.

"Did any of you gentlemen want to argue with *me*?" roared Silver. "Take a cutlass, him that dares, and I'll see the red of his insides!"

Not a man stirred. Not a man answered.

There was a long pause, then the men got together at the far end of the

log-house, whispering to each other and looking at Silver.

"You seem to have a lot to say," remarked Silver. "Speak up, and let me hear it!"

"This crew's dissatisfied," said one. "This crew has rights like any other crew, and I claim my right to step outside and talk there."

He gave a sea-salute and calmly walked from the house. One by one, the others followed him, each making a salute. Soon, Silver and I were left alone.

"You're within half a plank of death, Jim Hawkins," he whispered. "They're going to stop me being captain, but I'll stand by you."

"You mean all is lost?" I said.

"Ay, I do!" he answered. "Once I looked into the bay and saw the ship was gone, I knew it was the end. I'll save your life if I can, but you must save Long John from the hangman."

"I'll do what I can," I said.

"I know you've got that ship safe somewhere," he said. "But there's trouble nearer at hand. And talking of trouble, why did the doctor give me the map, Jim?" I looked so surprised to hear this that he knew I didn't have an answer. "Ah, well, he did. And there must be a reason, bad or good."

The door opened and a group of pirates stood together, just inside. One was pushed forward to speak for the others.

"Step up, lad," cried Silver. "I won't eat you!"

The man gave something to Silver. The sea-cook looked at it.

"The black spot! I thought so," he said.

A tall man with yellow eyes spoke next. "This crew has tipped you the black spot, John Silver," he said. "Turn it over and see what's written there; then you can talk."

"Thank you, George," said Silver. "What does it say? Ah! Removed from being cap'n eh? Why you're getting to be quite a leading man here, George. You'll be cap'n next, I shouldn't wonder. But I'm still your cap'n until I hear your grievances, and meantime your black spot ain't worth a biscuit."

"Listen," replied George. "First, you've made a hash of this cruise. Second, you let the enemy out of this trap for nothing. Third, you wouldn't let us attack them on the march. And fourth, there's this boy."

"Is that all?" said Silver. "Then I'll answer you. Made a hash of the cruise, did I? You all know what I wanted, and if that had been done we'd be aboard the *Hispaniola* now, with the treasure in the hold, by thunder! And the boy? You want him dead. Well, isn't he a hostage? And are we going to waste a hostage? No, not when he might be our last chance! And why didn't we kill the others? You've been glad enough to have a doctor coming to see you every day – you

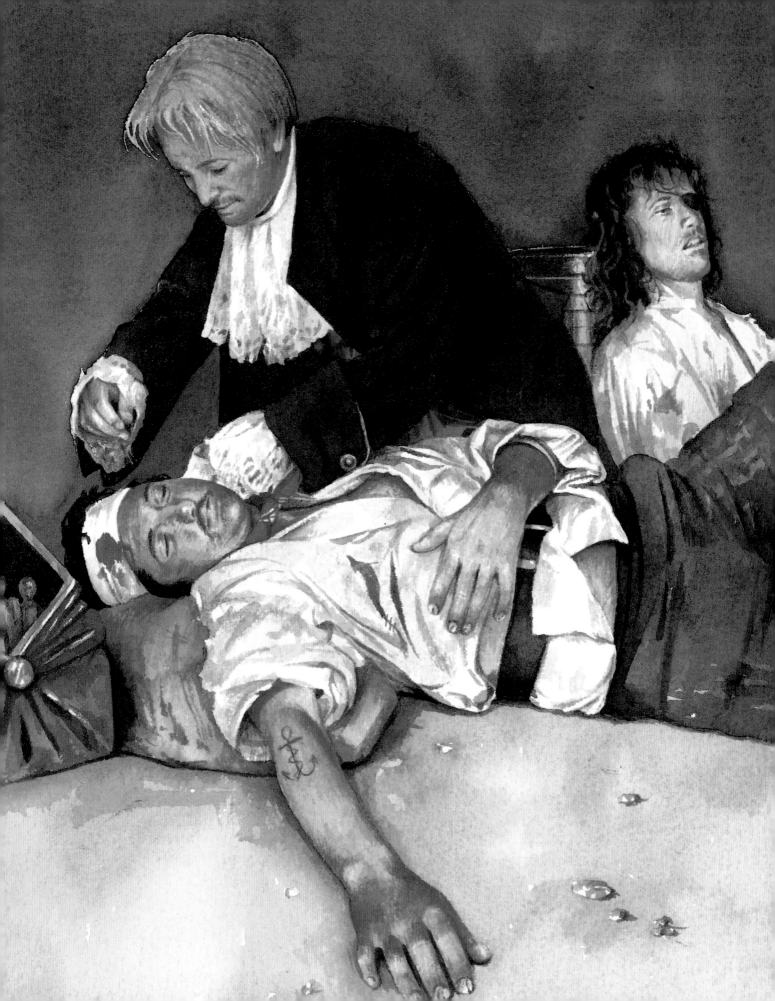

with your broken head, John, or you with the fever only six hours ago, George Merry. Why did I let them go? I made a bargain with them, that's why!"

He threw a piece of paper on to the floor. It was the map! But why had the doctor given it to him? I wondered.

The pirates jumped on it like cats upon a mouse.

"Very pretty," said George Merry. "But how are we to get the treasure away, us with no ship?"

"How do I know?" shouted Silver. "You and the others lost the ship and I found the treasure. Now I resign as cap'n. So choose whom you please, I'm done with it!"

"Silver!" they cried. "Silver for ever!"

"So that's the tune, is it?" said Silver. He smiled. "George, I reckon you'll have to wait another turn, my friend."

Dr. Livesey came early the next morning.

"Top o' the morning to you, doctor," said Silver. "We've got a surprise for you. We've a little stranger here."

By this time, the doctor was inside the stockade and I could hear his voice. "Not Jim?" he said.

"The very same Jim as ever was," replied Silver.

The doctor stopped. "Well, well," he said at last. "Duty first and pleasure afterwards. Let's look at these patients of yours, Silver."

He entered the house and, with one grim nod at me, went on with his work among the sick. He did not seem the least afraid, yet he must have known his life was in danger among these treacherous men.

"Well, that's done for today," he said, after giving each man what medicine he needed. "And now I wish to talk with that boy, please."

George Merry was at the door. "No!" he cried.

"Silence!" roared Silver. "Doctor," he went on in his usual voice. "I was thinking of that, and I believe I've found a way that will suit us all. Hawkins, will you give me your word of honour as a young gentleman that you will not escape?"

I promised.

"Doctor, you just step outside that stockade," said Silver, "and I'll bring the boy down on the inside. You can talk through the fence."

The men's anger exploded immediately after the doctor left the house. Silver was accused of making a separate peace for himself, but he called them fools and waved the map in their faces.

"Can we afford to break the peace on the very day we're going treasure hunting?" he cried. "No, by thunder! We'll break it when the right time

comes." And he stalked out on his crutch, his hand on my shoulder. "Slowly, lad," he whispered. "We mustn't be seen to hurry."

Dr. Livesey was waiting on the other side of the stockade, and when we were within speaking distance, Silver stopped.

"This boy will tell you how I saved his life," said Silver. "Doctor, you'll say a good word for me?"

"Why, John, you're not afraid?" asked Dr. Livesey.

"Doctor, I'm no coward!" said Silver. "But I'll admit the thought of the gallows makes me shake. You're an honourable man, and you'll not forget the good I've done, so I'll step aside and leave you and Jim alone."

When Silver was out of earshot, the doctor spoke. "So, Jim," he said, sadly, "here you are. I cannot find it in my heart to blame you, but this I must say: when Captain Smollett was well, you dared not leave; but when he was wounded and couldn't stop you, then you ran away. It was downright cowardly."

I began to cry. "Doctor," I said, "I've blamed myself enough."

"Jim," said the doctor, his voice changed. "Jim, I can't have this. Jump over and we'll run for it!"

"No," I said. "I gave my word, and Silver trusted me. I must go back. But, doctor, you didn't let me finish. I got the ship, partly by luck and partly by daring, and she lies beached in the North Inlet."

"The ship!" exclaimed the doctor.

Rapidly, I told him of my adventures and he listened in silence.

Then he said, "It's you that saved our lives, Jim. Do you suppose we're going to let you lose yours? Silver!" he called, and when the cook drew near again, said, "I'll give you some advice. Don't be in any hurry to find that treasure. And look out for squalls when you find it."

"What are you after?" said Silver. "Why have you given me the map?"

"I've no right to say more," said the doctor. "It's not my secret, or I'd tell it. But if we both get out of this alive, Silver, I'll do my best to save you. My second piece of advice is, keep the boy close beside you, and when you need help, give a shout."

Dr. Livesey shook hands with me through the stockade, nodded to Silver, and set off at a brisk pace into the wood.

Treasure Hunt

"JIM," said Silver, when we were alone, "if I saved your life, you've saved mine, and I'll not forget it. I saw the doctor wave his arm and tell you to run for it, and I saw you shake your head and say no. Now, we'll stick close together like the doctor said, and save our necks somehow."

Just then, a man shouted to say breakfast was ready, and we went back to eat it with the others.

Silver sat with Captain Flint on his shoulder. "It's lucky you have me to think for you, mates," he told them. "I got what I wanted. Sure enough, they have the ship. Where they have it, I don't know yet. But once we have the treasure we'll find it. As for our hostage, I'll keep him close to me when we go treasure-hunting, and once we've got both ship and treasure we'll talk Mr. Hawkins into joining us, we will, and give him his share for all his kindness."

The men were happy, but I was afraid. Silver was already a traitor twice over, and, if his plan proved workable, I had no doubt he would forget about Dr. Livesey and the others. He would prefer wealth and freedom with the pirates to barely escaping the hangman, which would be the best we could offer him on our side.

And even if he was forced to keep his promise to Dr. Livesey, what danger lay before us! A boy and a cripple against five strong seamen!

There was also the mysterious behaviour of my friends to worry me. Why had they given up the stockade so easily? Why had they parted with the map? And what had Dr. Livesey meant when he'd told Silver to 'look out for squalls' when we found the treasure?

After breakfast, we set out on our hunt, a strange-looking bunch in ragged and dirty sailors' clothes, and all armed to the teeth except me. Silver had two guns, besides the great cutlass at his waist, and a pistol in each pocket of his coat. Captain Flint sat on his shoulder, gabbling away. I had a rope around my waist and followed the sea-cook, who held the other end. Some of the men carried picks and shovels, others carried food.

We walked to the beach, where two small boats awaited us. The men discussed the contents of the map. The red cross was far too large to be a guide, and the words on the back of the map were not much help either.

Tall tree, Spyglass Shoulder, bearing a point to the N of NNE.
Skeleton Island ESE and by E.
Ten feet.

We landed the boats at the mouth of the second river, then began to climb Spyglass Hill. The group spread itself out in a fan shape, shouting and leaping to and fro. Silver and I followed a good way behind the rest, me at the end of my rope and he slithering and sliding on the marshy ground. From time to time I had to lend him a hand or he would have fallen backward down the hill.

We had gone about half a mile and were appoaching the brow of the hill when a man cried out, as if in terror. The others started to run towards him.

"He can't have found the treasure," said old Morgan, hurrying past us. "That's at the top."

Indeed, as we discovered when we reached the spot, it was something very

different. At the foot of a tall pine tree lay a human skeleton, a few shreds of clothing still clinging to it. Cold fear struck the heart of every man who saw it.

"He was a seaman," said George Merry who, bolder than the rest of us, was examining the rags of clothing. "This is good sea-cloth."

"Ay, you're right," said Silver. "But what sort of way is that for bones to lie? It isn't natural."

The skeleton lay perfectly straight, its feet pointing one way, its hands, raised above his head, pointing in the opposite direction.

"I've had an idea," said Silver. "Here's the compass, and there's the tip-top point of Skeleton Island, sticking out like a tooth. Just take a bearing along the lines of those bones."

It was done. The body pointed straight in the direction of the island, and the compass read ESE and by E.

"I thought so," said Silver. "This is a pointer. Right up there is our line for the treasure. But, by thunder, it makes me cold inside to think of Flint using a dead man to point the way."

When we reached the top of the hill, Silver sat down and took certain bearings with his compass.

"There are three 'tall trees'," he said, "in about the right line from Skeleton Island. 'Spyglass Shoulder' must mean that lower point there. It'll be child's play to find the treasure now."

Suddenly, out of the middle of the trees in front of us, a thin, high, trembling voice began to sing the well-known words:

> "Fifteen men on The Dead Man's Chest –
> Yo-ho-ho, and a bottle of rum!"

The effect on the pirates was dreadful to watch. Their faces drained and some jumped to their feet while some caught hold of others. Morgan grovelled on the ground.

"It's Flint!" cried George Merry.

The song had stopped as suddenly as it had begun.

"This won't do," said Silver, struggling to get the words out. "I can't put a name to the voice, but it's somebody skylarking about – and it's no ghost, either!"

Then the voice broke out again. "Darby M'Graw!" it wailed. "Darby M'Graw! Darby M'Graw! Fetch the rum, Darby!"

The pirates stood rooted to the ground, their eyes bulging in their heads, as the voice died away.

"That does it!" gasped one. "Let's go!"

"They were Flint's last words!" moaned Morgan.

Silver made a great effort to calm himself enough to speak. "Shipmates," he cried. "I'm here to get that treasure, and I'll not be beaten by man or ghost. I never feared Flint when he was alive, and I'll face him dead, by thunder! There's seven hundred thousand pounds not a quarter of a mile from here. When did a gentleman of fortune ever leave that amount of money for a boozy old seaman – and him dead, too?"

The others were too terrified to reply. They would have run away if they had dared, but fear kept them together.

"And another thing," went on Silver. "There was an echo. Now, no man ever saw a ghost with a shadow, so what's it doing with an echo, I'd like to know? That ain't natural."

George Merry relaxed a little. "That's so," he said. "Come to think ot it, it was like Flint's voice, I grant you, but not exactly like it. It was like somebody else's voice. More like – "

"Ben Gunn!" roared Silver.

"Ay, so it was!" cried Morgan.

"It makes no odds, does it?" said Dick. "Ben Gunn's not here in body any more than Flint is."

The others were scornful.

"Nobody minds Ben Gunn," cried George Merry, "dead or alive!"

They became more cheerful at this thought. We walked on, Merry going ahead with Silver's compass to keep us on the right line with Skeleton Island.

We reached the first of the tall trees, but it was the wrong one. So was the second. The third rose nearly two hundred feet into the air and could be seen far out to sea, both from the east and the west. But it was not its size that impressed the pirates, it was the thought that seven hundred thousand pounds lay buried somewhere beneath its spreading branches. The thought of this money swallowed up their fears; their eyes grew brighter, their feet speedier. They could not wait to get their hands on the treasure.

Silver hobbled, grunting, on his crutch. He pulled furiously on the rope that held me to him, and from time to time he turned and stared at me with a deadly look. I could read his thoughts easily. Now that we were so near the gold, all else had been forgotten. His promise and the doctor's warning were both things of the past. I knew that he hoped to seize the treasure, cut every honest throat on that island, find and board the *Hispaniola* under cover of night, and sail away with all his riches, leaving a trail of murder behind him.

It was hard for me to keep up with the rapid pace of the treasure-hunters.

Now and again I stumbled so that Silver had to pull roughly at the rope to drag me on.

We were now at the edge of the thicket.

"All together, mates!" shouted George Merry, and the men began to run.

Suddenly, not ten yards farther, we saw them stop. A low cry went up. Silver doubled his pace, digging away with the foot of his crutch like a madman. The next moment we were with them.

Before us was a great hole. It was not a very recent one for the sides had fallen in and grass had sprouted at the bottom. On the floor of the hole lay a broken pick and some wood from several packing cases.

It was quite clear. The hiding place had been found and the treasure taken. The seven hundred thousand pounds had gone!

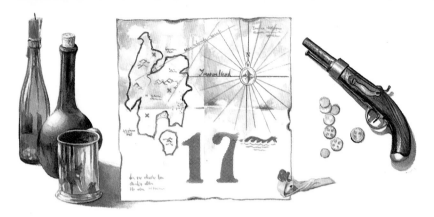

Saved!

THE pirates were shocked, each man looking as though he had been struck. But Silver recovered quickly and changed his plan before the others had time to realise their disappointment.

"Jim," he whispered, "take that, and stand by for trouble."

And he passed me a double-barrelled pistol.

At the same time he began to move quietly, and after a few steps had put the hollow between us two and the other five. His looks were quite friendly towards me now, and I couldn't help whispering, "So you've changed sides again!"

There was no time for him to answer. The buccaneers, with oaths and cries, leapt into the pit, one after the other. They began to dig with their fingers, throwing the wood to one side. Morgan found a piece of gold and held it up. It was a two-guinea piece and was passed among them.

"Two guineas!" roared George Merry, shaking it at Silver. "That's your seven hundred thousands pounds, is it? You're the man for bargains, are you? You're the man who never bungled anything, are you?"

"Standing for cap'n again, Merry?" said Silver.

But this time every one agreed with Merry and began to scramble out of the hole on the opposite side from us. There we stood, two on one side, five on the other, and the pit between us. Silver watched them, looking as cool as ever. He was brave, and no mistake.

"Mates!" cried Merry. "There's two of them alone there. The old cripple who brought us here all for nothing, and that boy who I'm going to have the heart out of! Now, mates – "

He was raising his arm and his voice, ready to lead a charge. But just then – CRACK! CRACK! CRACK! – three musket shots came from the thicket. Merry tumbled head-first into the hole, and another spun round and fell on his side, where he lay dead but still twitching. The other three turned and ran for their lives.

A moment later, Dr. Livesey, Gray and Ben Gunn joined us, guns still

smoking, from among the trees.

"Forward!" cried the doctor. "Double quick, my lads. We must head 'em off the boats!"

We set off at a great pace, sometimes plunging waist-deep through the bushes. Silver was anxious to keep up, leaping with his crutch, but was thirty yards behind us when we reached the brow of the hill.

"Doctor!" he cried. "There's no hurry! Look!"

And sure enough, he was right. In a more open part, we could see the three survivors still running in the same direction as they had started, towards Mizzenmast Hill. We were already between them and the boats. So we sat down to rest while Long John, mopping his face, caught up with us.

"Thank you, Doctor," he said. "You came in the nick of time for me and Hawkins. And so it's you, Ben Gunn!" he added. "Well, you're a nice one, to be sure."

The doctor sent Gray back for one of the pirates' pick-axes, dropped in their flight, and then we walked downhill to where the boats were lying. As we walked, the doctor told us Ben Gunn's story. Ben was the hero from beginning to end.

In his lonely wanderings round the island, Ben had found the skeleton, then found the treasure and dug it up. He had carried it to a cave on the northeast corner of the island two months before the *Hispaniola* arrived. Dr. Livesey had got this secret out of Ben on the afternoon of the attack. The next day, when the doctor saw that the ship had gone, he went to Silver and gave him the map – which was now useless – and handed over the stores – which did not matter because Ben Gunn's cave was well-stocked with food.

That morning – when he learned that I was going to be with the pirates when they discovered that the treasure had gone – he had run all the way to Ben's cave and, leaving the squire to look after the captain, took Gray and Ben with him to try and help us. He quickly saw that we were well ahead of him, and sent Ben Gunn on in front to do what he could. Ben had succeeded in delaying the pirates by playing ghost long enough for the doctor and Gray to catch up and to get ready for the ambush at the pine tree.

"Ah," said Silver, "so it was fortunate for me that I had Hawkins here. Otherwise you would have let old John be cut to pieces without a thought, doctor."

The doctor said quite cheerfully that Silver was right.

By this time, we had reached the boats. The doctor smashed one of them

with the pick-axe. Then we all got aboard the other and rowed towards the North Inlet. The *Hispaniola* was afloat now, the tide high enough to take her off the beach. We went round to Rum Cove, the nearest point for Ben Gunn's treasure-house. Gray returned to the *Hispaniola* alone to guard the ship overnight.

Squire Trelawney was at the cave to meet us. He said nothing to me of my running away, but when Silver saluted him, the squire became red in the face.

"John Silver," he said, "you're a villain and an imposter, sir! I have been told not to prosecute you, and I will not, but dead men's ghosts will haunt you!"

The cave was a large, airy place, with a little spring and a pool of clear water, and a floor of sand. Captain Smollett lay in front of a big fire, and in a far corner I could see great heaps of coins and gold bars. There lay Flint's treasure that we had come so far to find, and which had cost the lives of seventeen men from the *Hispaniola*. And how many others? I wondered. How much blood had been shed for it, how much sorrow, how many lies told? Perhaps no man alive could tell.

I ate a good supper that night with all my friends around me. Never, I am sure, were people happier. And there was Silver, eating heartily.

"What brought you back here, man?" the captain asked him.

"I came back to do my duty, sir," replied Silver.

"Ah!" said the captain, and that was all he said.

End of the Adventure

NEXT morning, we began early. Moving the great mass of gold a mile overland and then three miles by boat to the *Hispaniola* was hard work for so small a number of men.

The three pirates still on the island did not trouble us. They'd had enough of fighting. We held a meeting to decide what to do about them. In the end, it was decided that we would leave them on the island with a good supply of food, powder and medicine, together with a few tools, rope and extra clothing.

At last, one fine morning, we sailed out of North Inlet and headed for the nearest port in Spanish America, for we could not risk a voyage home without a fresh crew. Before noon, to my great joy, the highest rock of Treasure Island had disappeared below the blue horizon. I never wanted to see it again.

It was just at sundown that we dropped anchor at a beautiful harbour, and were immediately surrounded by people in small boats. They were happy to see us and, when the doctor, the squire and I rowed ashore, they offered to sell us fruit and vegetables.

Business ashore took some time, and it was daybreak the next morning before we returned to the *Hispaniola*. Ben Gunn greeted us with the news that Long John Silver had gone, sneaking off when Ben had briefly gone ashore.

The sea-cook had not gone empty-handed. He had taken one of the sacks of coin, worth perhaps three or four hundred guineas. But I think we were pleased to be rid of the villain at so small a price.

We found a crew at that port, then made a good voyage home. Only five of the men who had sailed from Bristol came back with the *Hispaniola*. 'Drink and the devil had done for the rest' with a vengeance.

All of us had a good share of the treasure – some of us using it wisely, others foolishly. Captain Smollett is now retired from the sea. Gray not only saved his money but is now mate and part-owner of a fine ship, and married with a family. As for Ben Gunn, he got a thousand pounds, which he spent or lost in just nineteen days, and was back begging for work on the twentieth! He was given a job as the squire's gatekeeper.

Of Silver we have heard no more. That fearful seaman with one leg has at last gone out of my life. Nothing would make me go back to that ill-fated island. And my worst dreams are when I hear the surf booming about its coasts, or when I wake up with the sharp voice of Captain Flint still ringing in my ears. "Pieces of eight! Pieces of eight!"